My Sister, *My Science Report*

My Sister,
My Science Report

BY MARGARET BECHARD

VIKING

VIKING
Published by the Penguin Group
Viking Penguin, a division of Penguin Books USA Inc.,
40 West 23rd Street, New York, New York 10010, U.S.A.
Penguin Books Ltd, 27 Wrights Lane, London W8 5TZ, England
Penguin Books Australia Ltd, Ringwood, Victoria, Australia
Penguin Books Canada Ltd, 2801 John Street, Markham, Ontario, Canada L3R 1B4
Penguin Books (N.Z.) Ltd, 182–190 Wairau Road, Auckland 10, New Zealand

Penguin Books Ltd, Registered Offices: Harmondsworth, Middlesex, England

First published in 1990 by Viking Penguin, a division of Penguin Books USA Inc.
10 9 8 7 6 5 4 3 2 1
Copyright a Margaret E. Bechard, 1990
All rights reserved

LIBRARY OF CONGRESS CATALOGING IN PUBLICATION DATA
Bechard, Margaret E.   my sister, my science report
    Margaret E. Bechard.   p.   cm.
    Summary: Though Tess is stuck with the class nerd for a partner in
a science project, they become good friends as they study the
unlikely subject of Tess's older sister.
    ISBN 0-670-83290-1
    [1. Science projects—Fiction.   2. Schools—Fiction.   3. Sisters—
Fiction.]   I. Title.
PZ7.B38066My   1990   [Fic]—dc20   89-24842

Printed in the United States of America
Set in Aster

For Alex, who read it;
for Nicholas, who told everybody about it;
and for Peter, who doesn't like chapter books.
And, always, for Lee,
who knows computers and constellations.

Contents

My Sister, *My Science Report*

The Worst Thing

I banged open the door and stomped into the kitchen.

Dad turned from the sink and said, "Good morning to you, too, Tess."

Mom glanced up from the crossword puzzle. "It's Saturday. I thought you'd be watching cartoons for another two hours."

"I'm too depressed," I said. I slumped into my

chair and sighed. No one said anything. I sighed again, loudly. No one said anything. "This is the worst day of my life, you know," I said.

"How do you know it's the worst day of your life if it's only ten o'clock in the morning?" Dad took a plate of muffins out of the microwave and put it on the table.

"Ten o'clock and the phone hasn't rung yet?" Mom said. "Amazing."

The phone rang.

Dad answered it. "It's for you, Tess. Melissa Fried-Bacon."

"Field-Eaton," I corrected automatically.

"Hi, Tess." In the background, I could hear the theme song to "The Goops." I was missing all the good TV shows. Melissa sounded like she was eating breakfast. "I just wanted to remind you to watch 'Captain Cosmo' this afternoon. He'll be drawing for the grand prize, the trip to Enchanted Mountain. I just know one of us will win this time."

"Melissa," I said, in a voice so heavy with disgust I got spit all over the telephone, "I have other things to think about today than 'Captain Cosmo.'"

"Oh. Yeah. I forgot. Gee, Tess, that sure was nasty

of Mr. Sanders to make you be Phoenix Guber's partner. And in front of the whole class, too."

"It was the worst thing anybody's ever done to me. He used to be my favorite teacher. I can't believe he did this to me. Phoenix Guber. Coming to my house for the whole day." I moaned and rested my head against the kitchen cabinet.

"I was going to pick you for my partner, Tess, I really was. I have to have Michael for a partner. We have to spend all of tomorrow afternoon on our report." But she didn't sound too sad about it. And why should she? Michael is cute, funny, and goes to gymnastics class. He is not a total space case. And there is nothing good on television on Sunday afternoon.

The music from her TV changed. "Oh-oh. 'Marauding Tortoises from Space' is starting. I really have to go. Don't forget about 'Captain Cosmo,' okay?"

"I won't." I hung the phone up slowly, sat down again, and put my head on the table.

The kitchen door swung open and my big sister, Jane, came in. She was still in the T-shirt she sleeps in. Her hair was sticking up all over the place and she had globs of acne medicine on her face. She was carrying our cat, Oscar Wilde. If I hadn't been so miserable, I would have asked her where her broom was.

The really unfair thing was that Jane actually didn't look that bad. Jane almost always looks good. Sometimes, she even looks great. It's the long, wavy blond hair and the big blue eyes. My hair is straight, brown, and boring. My mother says my eyes are hazel which means, basically, that they're brown. Sometimes, I look pretty good. Mostly, I just look ordinary.

Jane put Oscar down next to his bowl. "What's wrong with Tess the Mess?" she asked.

"None of your business!" I shouted.

"Who exactly is Phoenix Guber, anyway?" Dad asked, buttering a muffin. "And why is he coming to our house?"

"Phoenix Guber!" Jane shrieked. She collapsed into a chair. "Coming to our house to see Tess?" She burst out laughing.

Mom pushed the muffins toward her. "Eat your breakfast, Jane. Phoenix is a perfectly nice boy in Tess's class. They're going to do a science report together. He's coming over this morning to work on it."

"He's not perfectly nice," I said. "He's perfectly awful. Everybody calls him Phoenix Boober. He looks funny and he smells funny and he acts dumb. He knocks stuff over all the time and spills things. On Tuesday, he spilled a whole thing of paint on Melissa's new sneakers and yesterday he spent fifteen minutes talking about the red spot on Jupiter when Mr. Sanders asked him the capital of Oregon. Nobody in the whole class likes him. Why did Mr. Sanders have to pick me to be his partner?"

"Don't judge a book by its cover, Tess," Jane said, in that fake-adult voice she's been using the past few months.

Mom put a muffin on Jane's plate. "Eat your breakfast," she said again.

"It sounds to me like that's the only way this poor kid could get a partner," Dad said.

"But why does it have to be me? It's not fair. Melissa and I had it all planned. We were going to work together."

"What would you and Melissa do a project on?" Jane asked. "Cartoon shows?"

"We were going to do a project on raccoons," I said. "You know, because of the one that's always knocking over our garbage can?"

"Speaking of which," Mom said, pointing her buttery knife at the back door.

"See?" I said. "It would have been perfect. And then . . . and then . . ." I could feel the tears brimming up to the edges of my eyes. "Then Mr. Sanders said I had to be Phoenix's partner. And everybody in the room laughed." The tears came too fast and started running down the sides of my nose.

Mom handed me a napkin. "Here. Your muffin will get soggy."

"Phoenix Guber," Jane said. "Tess is doing a project with Phoenix Guber." She shook her head and laughed.

"Jane," Mom said.

"What a name," Dad said. "What were his parents thinking of?"

"Obviously not English literature," Mom said.

"Vancouver Guber," Jane said. "That would have sounded better."

Dad laughed.

Jane laughed, too. "Or maybe," she said, "maybe Melissa Field-Eaton could lend him one of her names. She's got way too many."

"You leave my friends alone!" I shouted.

"I didn't know Phoenix was one of your friends."

"He's not. I hate him. He's a goon."

"Tess, you will not call people goons." Dad started clearing the table. "What is this science report on, anyway?" He put down the plate he had just picked up and leaned over the table toward me. "Put it to me straight, Tess. You don't need a costume, do you? You don't have to dress up as a Bunsen burner or anything?"

I was just about to ask him what a Bunsen burner was, when I caught myself. My father is very good at getting you off the track.

"This is serious, Daddy. I don't think any of you are taking this seriously!"

"We're sorry, Tess," Mom said. "What are you and Phoenix doing your report on?"

"Barn owls," I said, sighing. "Mr. Sanders let Phoenix pick and he picked barn owls. I hate barn owls. Their faces look like sliced bananas and they eat baby mice." I turned to my mother and clasped my hands together. "Mom. Please. Please call Mr. Sanders and tell him I have to be Melissa's partner. Please, please, please."

Mom and Dad looked at each other over my head. Jane was leaning back in her chair, enjoying the whole thing.

"Barn owls are really interesting birds, Tess," she said. "We studied them in Natural History."

"That's right, Tess," Dad said. "You may find out you like barn owls."

"But Melissa and I would do it on something we both like. We both like raccoons already."

"Tess," Mom said. "You and Melissa are together enough already. I think it will be good for you to work with Phoenix." She leaned over and whispered: "And I think it will be good for Phoenix to work with you."

I moaned. Across the table, Jane smiled her tight little smile that doesn't show her braces. Slowly, very slowly, her mouth started moving. No sound came out, but I could tell what she was saying: "Tess loves Phoenix."

"I do not! I hate him!"

Mom moaned and put her head down on the table.

"Have to make room for all these heads," Dad said, taking her plate away.

The doorbell rang.

"There, that's probably Phoenix now," Dad said.

"If he's really that smart," Mom said to the table-cloth, "he won't hang around here."

Jane grabbed her muffin and stood up. "Well, I think I'll go get dressed," she said. At the dining-room door, she turned back and made kissy faces at me.

"I'll . . . I'll . . ." I didn't know what I was going to do. "I'll get you, Jane!" I shouted, finally.

But she was gone.

The doorbell rang again.

Mom and Dad were looking at me.

I shoved my chair back and stomped out of the kitchen.

Better Than Kool-Aid

Seeing Phoenix Guber, in the flesh, on my front porch, did not make me feel better. He was wearing his NASA cap and the green backpack he even wears out to recess. He was carrying about fifty big, fat books. Big, fat books with boring brown covers probably filled with boring facts about boring barn owls.

"Good morning, Tess." One of the books thudded to the porch, missing his foot by about an inch.

"Don't you know it's rude to keep ringing and ringing someone's doorbell?" I shouted.

Phoenix blinked at me behind his thick glasses. "I guess I was just in a hurry to get started." Another book started to slide out of his arms but he caught it with his knee.

"Don't leave Phoenix out in the cold, Tess." My mother had snuck up behind me.

"Oh, I'm not cold, Mrs. Anderson. In fact, I'd say it's unseasonably warm for Oregon in April, wouldn't you?"

My mother nodded her head, slowly. "Yes. I guess I'd say that, Phoenix. Tess, help him with the books."

"I've got them, Mrs. Anderson. I'm used to handling books." Somehow he juggled the books in his arms, picked up the one he'd dropped, and stepped into the house. Usually Phoenix can't even walk and talk at the same time.

"Wait!" I hadn't heard my mother's voice squawk like that since the time my father knocked over the china cabinet with the Christmas tree. "Your boots!"

We all looked at Phoenix's feet. He was wearing

black rubber boots, the kind firemen and kinder-
gartners wear. Mud was dripping off them onto the
hardwood floor.

"Gee, Mrs. Anderson. I'm sorry." Phoenix bent
down to take off the boots and dropped all the books
with an enormous crash.

Dad's head poked out of the kitchen for a second,
then disappeared.

Mom looked at me. I leaned against the wall,
smiled, and shrugged. I'd warned her. It was good
for her to see Phoenix in action. Maybe she'd call
Mr. Sanders before the entire house became a dis-
aster area.

She frowned at me and smiled at Phoenix. "It's
all right. We can clean that up in a jiffy." My
mother, as a rule, does not use words like "jiffy."
She pointed outside. "Take them off on the porch.
What happened to you?"

"I was over by the Wilsons' looking for owl pellets
near their barn and I guess I kind of ended up in
the creek."

The boots made sucking noises as Phoenix pulled
them off. "I did find a nice owl pellet, though." He
wiped his muddy hands on his pants and dug into

one of his lumpy pockets. Only Phoenix Guber actually puts things in the pockets of his cargo pants. He pulled out two rocks, something that looked like a bone, and, finally, a wad of fuzzy black stuff. I hated to think what might be in the other pockets.

He held the fuzzy wad out to my mother.

She took a step backward. "Oh . . . well . . . isn't that . . ." She looked at me. I smiled again. She frowned again. "Just leave your boots and your . . . your pellet thing on the porch to dry out, Phoenix. You and Tess can work in the dining room."

"I'll keep the owl pellet," Phoenix said. "We'll need it."

He stepped back into the hall and Mom shut the door. His socks left wet tracks. Mom bit her lip. "Help Phoenix pick up the books, Tess."

I picked up two and carried them to the dining-room table. They weighed a ton. Books that are all words and no pictures always weigh more. This was going to be even worse than I had thought. I slumped into a chair.

Phoenix brought in the other books. Then he took off his backpack, opened it up, and dumped about ten more books onto the table. He rooted around in the bottom of the backpack, pulled out a notebook and pencil, and carefully put the backpack back on.

He sat down and opened the notebook to a blank page. He wrote "Barn Owls" at the top and underlined it twice. Then he adjusted the strap that holds his glasses on. His sandy blond hair stuck straight out between the strap and the bottom of his cap.

He looked at me. "You'll need to take notes, Tess. There's a lot of information in these books."

"I know how to write a report, thank you, Phoenix."

Mom came out of the kitchen carrying a plate with the last of the muffins. "Here. These should help you keep up your strength." She smiled at me. I frowned at her.

"Have fun." She went back into the kitchen.

Phoenix put the owl pellet down next to the plate of muffins.

"Hey! Don't put that on the table!"

He stared at me. "Tess," he said in a slow, patient voice that made me want to punch him, "it's an owl pellet. You see, because owls often eat their prey whole, they have to regurgitate what they can't digest."

I stared at him. Raccoons do not do anything that disgusting.

Phoenix smiled at me. "Regurgitate means . . ."

"I know what it means, Phoenix. I just don't want that thing on our table. It's revolting."

He picked up the owl pellet. "I don't think it's revolting, Tess. I think it's fascinating. Did you know we should be able to get the entire skeleton of a small mammal out of this? We can then infer something about the owl's diet, about its habitat, about its hunting grounds. . . ."

"There's probably a little dead baby mouse in there, Phoenix, and that is revolting. And disgusting."

He opened his mouth like he was going to say something, then shut it. He shoved the owl pellet into one of his pockets. Then he rubbed his nose under his glasses, adjusted the strap again, and settled the glasses against his nose. "Look. Let's just get started. The sooner we get started, the sooner we can both be done. I know neither of us is very happy about this."

"Why aren't you happy? You got to pick the topic and everything."

He shoved at his cap and his right ear popped out. "But it's a totally ridiculous assignment. I mean, it's due Monday! We can't possibly do any kind of reasonable report when there's no time for on-site observation and research."

And we have to waste a perfectly good Saturday, I thought.

Phoenix jabbed at the paper with his pencil. "I really used to think that Mr. Sanders was my favorite teacher, but this is absolutely unfair."

I sat up straight. "Funny, I was saying the same thing just a little while ago."

"First of all, he limited the number of topics."

I nodded.

"Then he insisted we had to have partners."

I nodded again.

"And then he wouldn't even let us choose our own partners. I mean, I never would have chosen *you*."

I stopped in mid-nod. Wait a minute. I'd make a great partner. Anybody in the class would be thrilled to have me as a partner.

Phoenix leaned closer to me. "You know what I suspect, Tess? I suspect that the whole point of this is not even science. There's absolutely nothing scientific about it." He shoved at one of the books and it toppled to the other side of the table. "Scientists do not sit and read books and write a report."

I took a muffin. He was winding up. I could tell. "Please don't start on the red spot on Jupiter, okay? I just can't take that this morning."

He reached for a muffin and started peeling off the paper. "I'm not talking about Jupiter. I'm talking about science. Pure science. Real science."

Oscar Wilde walked under the table. I moved my feet before he could take a swipe at them. Oscar jumped into Phoenix's lap. Phoenix offered him the muffin, then took a bite himself.

"Real scientists go out into the field, not into a dining room," he said around the muffin bite. "To do a real study of barn owls, we'd need to build a blind in the Wilsons' barn and sit there, day and night, for months, watching the owls in their natural habitat."

I shuddered. "Phoenix. I don't want to sit in a smelly old barn and watch owls spit. Besides, my mother wouldn't let me."

He sat back and rubbed Oscar's head. "Mine probably wouldn't either. But it's still not fair. How can Mr. Sanders expect us to do a book report and call it science?"

Jane clumped down the stairs. She had on a sweatsuit and she had washed her face.

"I'm going to kill you if you don't stop using up all the shampoo in this house, Tess," she said.

As if I was the one who had to wash my hair every day. "Mom said you have to stop saying you're going to kill me," I said.

Jane leaned across the table. "Well, I'll kill you if you tell her I said I'll kill you."

I gritted my teeth. "Well, I'll put Kool-Aid in your shampoo bottle."

"Well, I'll . . ." Jane stopped and looked at Phoenix. He was staring at both of us like we were a tennis match. Jane leaned over farther and patted me on the head. "I'm sorry, Tess. I forgot your boyfriend was here."

She was in the kitchen before I could get up and strangle her.

Phoenix was staring at me. "Who was that?"

"My sister. My stupid sister. Ignore her."

"Does she always act like that?"

"She didn't used to." For a second, I remembered

when Jane hadn't acted so mean, back when we used to make forts out of the blankets and spend Saturday mornings watching TV together. It made me sort of sad, but not sad enough to forget how mad I was. Boyfriend! What an awful thing to say.

Phoenix was staring at the kitchen door. "My mother says it's just a phase," I said. "She says it will go away. I hope Jane just goes away with it."

Jane came out of the kitchen. "I'm going to use Mom's shampoo and you can't have any," she said. She took a muffin off the plate. "How are the love-birds coming along?"

Phoenix adjusted his glasses. "Actually, it's barn owls. Lovebirds would be considered pets, I think, and Mr. Sanders . . ."

"Ignore her," I said, through my teeth.

Jane burst out into high-pitched laughter. She thinks she sounds like some movie star when she does that. "You're too cute," she said, shaking her head at Phoenix. She smiled at me. "I can tell you two are going to be really special together."

"Ignore her," I said again.

She sort of wiggled over to the hall door. She stopped, looked back over her shoulder, and made kissy faces. Then she started laughing again. I could hear her laughing all the way up the stairs.

I knew my face was bright red. I looked at Phoenix out of the corners of my eyes. He was looking down at Oscar. What I could see of his face was red, too.

I cleared my throat. "Hadn't we better get started?"

Phoenix was still looking at Oscar. "Now that would be an interesting scientific study," he said.

"The cat?"

"No. Your sister."

It took a second for my brain to catch up. "My sister? Jane?"

"Yes." Phoenix looked at me and his eyes were bright. "It would be perfect, Tess. She is an animal. And she certainly displays interesting behavior."

"Phoenix . . ."

"She'd be relatively easy to study because she can't fly away or burrow underground or anything."

"Phoenix . . ."

"We could do on-site observation here in your own house." He pointed his finger at me. "No smelly barns, Tess."

"Phoenix. Shut up for just a minute. You're crazy.

Mr. Sanders would never let us do a science report on my sister."

Phoenix smiled a funny little smile and gently pulled at Oscar's ears. "Tess, you wouldn't believe what you can get away with once someone labels you talented and gifted. I bet Mr. Sanders would take a report on . . . on cartoon shows from me."

That was probably true. Phoenix got away with late papers and half-done homework all the time. There just might be advantages to having him as a partner. But . . . a science report on Jane?

"Phoenix, if Jane ever found out—I mean, if she knew we were doing a science report on her . . ." I couldn't even think what Jane would do. But I knew it would be ugly.

Phoenix glanced up at me from under the brim of his cap. He was grinning. "It would be better than Kool-Aid in her shampoo, Tess."

I watched Phoenix doodle for a minute and thought about it. I thought about all the times Jane had yelled at me and teased me and told me I was stupid. I thought about what a total jerk she had been for the past few months. "I suppose," I said, slowly, "it would even be real science."

Phoenix's grin got wider. "On-site, in-depth research of a subject in its natural habitat. And a lot more fun than reading all these books," he added.

"A scientific study," I said.

"In the natural habitat."

"That would probably be the bathroom." We looked at each other. We both giggled. I didn't even know Phoenix Guber could giggle.

"It would be awfully hard to build a blind in the bathroom," he said, seriously.

"Especially when she's in the shower," I said. "How about her bedroom?"

"That's an interesting idea. In fact, I think it might be perfect."

"She might see us, though," I said, suddenly getting a little worried.

"Not," said Phoenix, "if we're in the closet."

Red Lips, Green Skin

"The closet?" My stomach kind of tightened, like maybe I'd eaten too many muffins.

"Sure. We'll be able to see her, but she won't be able to see us." Phoenix pushed Oscar Wilde off his lap. He scratched out "Barn Owls" at the top of the paper. "What shall we call this?"

"Uh . . . how about 'A Science Report?' "

"Tess. That doesn't tell you anything." He chewed on the end of the pencil. "How about this?"

I stood up so I could see over his shoulder. He wrote: "A Scientific Study of an Adolescent Human in Its Natural Habitat, Based on Observation and On-Site Research." He looked up at me. "What do you think?"

"Well. It's long enough."

My dad came out of the kitchen carrying a cup of coffee and the newspaper. "How's the report going?" he asked.

"Great," I said.

Phoenix covered the notebook with his arm. "We have the title."

"Often the hardest part," Dad said.

As soon as the TV clicked on in the living room, Phoenix stood up.

"Let's go," he whispered.

We tiptoed up the stairs. The shower was running in the bathroom. Over the beating of the water, we could hear Jane singing.

Phoenix stopped at the head of the stairs and wrote something in the notebook. "Vocalization," he whispered.

"Love calls," I whispered back. He wrote that down, too.

I led the way to Jane's room but, at the door, a funny thing happened. My hand just sort of froze halfway to the doorknob.

"What's wrong?"

"If she catches me in her room, she'll kill me. But, if she catches me in her closet, she'll really kill me."

"So. She won't catch you." Phoenix reached around me and pushed the door open. "Holy cow," he said.

Jane's room was a pit. It smelled like sweaty sneakers that had been dipped in perfume. She hadn't made her bed and clothes were thrown all over the place. Her desk was covered with little bottles and tubes, most of them with their tops off. She'd stuck stickers and pictures and things to the mirror above the desk so that only a little area in the middle was clear. Something red had spilled down the desk drawers and onto the carpet. Above her bed was a big poster of Clint Harmon, star of "Crime Wave." Personally, I think it's weird to have a picture of a guy old enough to be your father in your bedroom.

Phoenix was staring around the room like it was a pretty interesting habitat. He wasn't even writing anything down. I yanked at his arm. "Come on. The hot water will run out in a minute."

I pulled open the closet door.

"I don't believe it," Phoenix said. "There are more clothes in here."

"Believe it," I said. I crawled over shoes and boots and what felt like a tennis racket to the very back of the closet.

Phoenix pulled the door shut. Suddenly it was pitch black and hot. Something was poking me in the bottom. I pulled out a hiking boot and tossed it aside.

"Ouch!" Phoenix said.

"Sorry. I can't see anything."

"Me either. And I think I'm sitting on an ice skate." The door creaked open a crack and a slit of light fell into the darkness.

"Shut that door! She'll see us!"

"But we won't be able to see her. And, anyway, I can't write in the dark."

"Who cares about writing? I care about getting killed."

"But I have to take notes, Tess. A good scientist . . . ouch. . . . It *is* an ice skate. . . . A good scientist always keeps careful notes in case someone else wants to duplicate his research."

For a second, I pictured all these guys in white coats sitting in Jane's closet. I pressed my mouth against my knees to keep from laughing.

The shower went clunk, clunk. The water stopped. All the laughter and all my spit dried up at the same time. I tried to move farther back but I was already against the wall. My hand brushed against something fuzzy, something with hard button eyes. Jane's old bunny. I picked it up and hugged it tight.

The bedroom door opened and slammed shut. Phoenix moved closer to the crack. I could see him in the slit of light. He had the notebook out in front of him.

I could hear Jane walking around. A chair scraped. A drawer opened. A jar rattled. Jane started humming.

Phoenix was writing and I could hear the pencil scratching on the paper. I hoped Jane was making too much noise to hear anything. I felt kind of like you feel in a scary movie, scared and happy and excited all at the same time.

My feet were going to sleep. I crawled around, very carefully, so I could kneel. Then I wiggled closer to the door. I could just see over Phoenix's head.

Jane was sitting at her desk. I could see the back of her head and her wet hair, dripping onto her bathrobe.

Jane leaned closer to the mirror.

"Oh, Jane," she said. Her voice sounded funny, like she had a sore throat. "Jane. You're my dream come true."

Next to me, I felt Phoenix's shoulders shake. I stuffed the bunny into my mouth to keep my own laughter in.

"Your eyes are like . . . are like the night sky. No. . . . Your eyes are like tide pools. . . . No. . . . Your eyes are so blue."

I wiped at my eyes with the back of my hand. I needed to laugh so bad, it hurt. I clamped my teeth on the bunny's ear.

Jane's head tilted and her voice changed. "Oh, Robby, you say the most incredible things."

Phoenix's pencil scratched again.

"Jane," she said in the hoarse voice, "where have you been all my life?"

I rocked back a little on my knees. This was even better than I had expected.

Something scraped against the closet door and my breath caught in my throat. Someone started purring. For a second, I thought it was Jane. Then Oscar Wilde's paw appeared at the edge of the door. The paw pulled. The door swung wider.

I shuffled backward. Hangers rattled above me.

"Meow," Oscar said.

"Oscar Wilde," Jane said. "Are you in my closet again?"

Phoenix gasped and moved back, too. A dress fell off its hanger and onto his head.

Jane's chair scraped. Oscar meowed again. I shut my eyes.

"You'd better not be doing anything disgusting on my shoes, you stupid cat."

Footsteps started across the floor. I tried to make myself very, very small.

I felt cold air. I heard Phoenix groan. I opened my eyes.

Jane was standing in the doorway. Her eyes looked very big. Her lips looked very red. Her skin looked very green. And very shiny.

I blinked a couple of times. Jane's skin was definitely green.

She just stood there, staring at her dress covering Phoenix's head and shoulders, staring at Oscar Wilde sitting on her sneakers, staring at me.

Oscar Wilde shot out of the closet, his tail bushed out and his ears flat on his head.

Phoenix shot out after him. He pulled the dress off his head and threw it over Jane's. "Sorry!" he yelled. "Wrong closet! Run, Tess, run!"

I dropped the bunny and scrabbled over shoes and boots. As I reached the door, Jane got the dress off her head. Some of the green stuff had rubbed off, leaving white streaks on her face. Her mouth was still open. I could see her braces glinting in the light. I couldn't make a sound.

Jane could. The green skin stretched across her cheeks. Her red, red mouth opened wide. "MOTHER!" she screamed.

And Purple Hair

I took the stairs three at a time. As I ran through the front hall, I saw my mother coming across the dining room. My father started to get up from his chair in the living room. I headed straight for the door.

Phoenix was sitting on the porch, pulling on his boots. I leapt over him, slamming the door behind me. I jumped off the edge of the porch and dashed around the side of the house.

Phoenix was right behind me. He had the notebook in one hand and the pencil clenched between his teeth. He still had on the backpack, but his NASA cap was pushed all the way back on his head.

We took one look at each other and burst out laughing.

"I thought I was going to explode in there," Phoenix said. His face was red and his bangs were plastered to his forehead. He pulled the cap back down over his ears.

I nodded. I didn't have enough breath to talk.

He flipped to a new page of the notebook. "How do you want to classify that green skin?"

"Maybe it's all the trees around here," I gasped. "Maybe she's trying to blend in to her surroundings. You know, like a chameleon. The walls in her room are green, you know." I tapped my finger on the notebook. "Or maybe it's like rabbits, and things that turn different colors in the summer and winter. Maybe she's going to be green all spring."

Phoenix was writing ninety miles an hour. He was grinning. "Protective coloration. This is great. You're really good at this, Tess."

I *was* good at this. Maybe I'd be a scientist when I grew up instead of a film editor. I realized I was grinning, too. This day was turning out really different from what I had expected.

Phoenix was flipping through the notebook, marking pages with different titles. He wrote "Range" on one page, "Social Interactions" on another, and "Diet" on another.

"That will be a short one," I said. "Pizza and diet soda."

He wrote those down. "We'll leave some room, though, in case we observe her eating other things."

"I just hope she doesn't spit them back out," I said.

Phoenix turned back to the page marked "Vocalization." "We should really write that stuff down about her voice changing all the time. You know, the way it kept getting lower and higher."

"Oh, Jane," I said.

"Oh, Robby," Phoenix said.

We both started laughing again.

The front door opened. "Tess!" my mother shouted.

I flattened myself against the side of the house.

"Tess Anderson!" It was Jane. "I'm going to kill you. You come out here right now!"

Phoenix put his finger to his lips. He peeked around the corner.

"I can't believe what that kid gets away with in this house. It's not fair!" Jane was still shouting.

"Calm down." Mom was not exactly shouting but I could hear her really well. "I'm sure it was just some kind of misunderstanding."

"Ha!" Jane said.

Phoenix's hand was waving at me. I moved up behind him and looked over his head.

Jane and my mom were standing on the front porch. Jane had gotten dressed in record time. Her hair was still wet, but otherwise she looked perfect. Not that she would be seen in public if she didn't. She was wearing black tights and her new boots that she d gotten for her birthday. She was also wearing Mom's favorite sweater. Mom must be really upset.

Phoenix was writing again. He put his mouth up close to my ear and whispered: "No green skin. Purple hair."

He was right. Jane's hair was still pulled back in a ponytail, but now it shone purple in the sunlight.

"I'm not going to stay around here and be tortured," Jane said.

"Where are you going?"

"To the store. I'm out of shampoo, remember? And I need more mousse, too."

"Okay, but be back in a hour, please. Dad and I are going out and I need you to stay with Tess."

I groaned, softly.

Jane groaned, loudly. "When is she going to be old enough to baby-sit herself?"

"Soon, but right now I feel better with someone in charge. I'll pay you," my mother added.

"Oh, all right. But tell Tess the Pest and her dopey boyfriend to stay out of my closet."

I didn't look at Phoenix. He was busy writing. I hoped he'd missed the boyfriend remark.

"I'll talk to Tess," my mother said. I didn't like the tone of her voice.

"Okay. See you later." Jane started down the steps.

"Not later. In an hour!" Mom called.

"Okay." Jane pulled her headphones over her ears and walked down the driveway.

Mom started to turn toward us. Phoenix and I both leapt back.

"Tess! Where are you?"

I closed my eyes and prayed she wasn't mad enough to come looking.

"Tahiti," she said, suddenly. Then, much louder: "I'm taking the first plane to Tahiti!" The front door opened and slammed shut.

"Whew," Phoenix said, "that was close. Does your mom shout on your porch very often?"

I opened my eyes. "Not very often."

Phoenix was looking up at me. "She sounded really mad, Tess. Maybe we should go back to barn owls."

"Oh, it's no big deal." I really didn't want to go back to those books, although maybe I should be figuring out how *I* could get to Tahiti.

Phoenix shoved at his glasses and looked at the ground. "I'm really sorry I got you into trouble, Tess. I just thought . . . you know . . . it would be sort of fun . . ."

I punched him on the shoulder. "Come on, Phoenix. We can't let a little setback like this stop us. We're scientists. We're doing important research. Just think, if Einstein had given up just because an apple fell on his head, we'd never have gotten to the moon."

Phoenix rubbed his shoulder and grinned. "Right, Tess."

"So, what next?"

Phoenix tugged at his cap and straightened his backpack. "I think we should follow her. Maybe we'll learn something about her range and eating habits."

"More likely we'll learn something about makeup, but let's go."

We cut through the Bormans' yard to get to the corner. Jane was about halfway down Maple. We started after her, slowly.

"Try to look inconspicuous," Phoenix said.

"Incon—what?"

"Try not to attract attention."

I looked at his muddy boots and his bulging pockets. I looked at his cap pulled down over the tops of his ears. I looked at him trying to walk and write in his notebook at the same time. *I* was going to attract attention?

"Moose are awfully big animals," Phoenix said, still writing. "I wonder where she'll keep them."

"Moose?" I said stupidly. "What've moose got to do with this?"

"She said she was going to the store for moose." Phoenix grinned up at me.

I grinned back. I didn't even know Phoenix Guber could make jokes.

"She's getting mousse for her hair, dummy. That's what makes it purple. Unless she buys red or blue."

"What was the green stuff on her face, do you suppose?"

"Probably something for zits. Jane's real big on zits."

Phoenix nodded and wrote that down, too.

I looked up and skidded to a stop. Jane was standing on the corner, looking down Walnut Street, snapping her fingers and swinging her head. I dove under the big red rhododendron bush in Mrs. Ehrlich's front yard. Phoenix ducked behind a telephone pole.

Suddenly Jane turned and started walking down Walnut.

I crawled out from under the bush. Phoenix came out from behind the pole.

"That's not the way to the shopping center," Phoenix said. "Where's she going?"

We walked around the corner. Jane was walking right back toward us, fiddling with the radio dial and not looking where she was going.

We ran back around the corner. We both dove under the rhododendron.

We lay there, not saying anything, for a long time. No Jane appeared.

"Where is she?" I muttered.

"Maybe she really isn't going shopping."

"Believe me, when Jane is out of shampoo, she goes shopping."

Phoenix crawled out from under the bush, stood up, and ran to the stop sign. He held on to it and looked down the street. Suddenly, he pushed away from the post and ran back to the rhododendron.

He flopped down beside me, panting.

"She's . . . she's walking . . . up and down . . . in front of a house."

"Did she see you?"

"No. She's looking at the house." He got out the notebook. "I wonder if this is typical behavior."

"It's typical," I said.

Phoenix looked at me.

This was actually sort of embarrassing. I took a deep breath. "Jane is in love with Robert Field-Eaton," I said, very fast. "Melissa told me that she'd seen Jane walking up and down in front of their house, but I didn't really believe it." I didn't care what kind of phases I went through. I knew I would never do something so dumb.

Phoenix was writing in the notebook. "Does Robert like her?"

"Robert doesn't even know she's alive."

A car stopped at the corner, turned onto Maple, and drove off toward the shopping center. Almost immediately, Jane appeared. She was walking fast now. As she crossed the street, she broke into a run.

Phoenix scrambled up. "We're going to lose her! Hurry, Tess."

I wasn't in any hurry. Thinking of Jane making a fool of herself in front of Melissa Field-Eaton's house had reminded me of something. It had reminded me that I was making a fool of myself, too. I was out in public with Phoenix Guber! I remembered how the kids yesterday had laughed. I remembered Jane calling him my boyfriend. What if somebody saw me walking around with him on a Saturday morning? Anybody might think he was with me . . . or worse.

"Come on, Tess." Phoenix was already across the street. He stood on the opposite corner, jogging in place, his backpack flapping, his boots clumping.

I crossed the street. "Phoenix." I cleared my throat. "Phoenix. I think maybe I should go home."

"What?"

"I said I think maybe I should go home."

He ran his fingers under his glasses. "Gee, Tess, don't you want to see where she goes?"

"Phoenix. I know where she's going. She's going to Valu-Drug. She's going to buy some mousse and try out the perfume samples and look at the new issue of *Seventeen*."

"Maybe she'll eat something she's never eaten

before. Or maybe she'll engage in some new vocalization. Research in the field can be really surprising, Tess."

"Oh, don't be so weird, Phoenix."

I was sorry. Right away, as soon as I'd said it, I was sorry.

He looked at his boots, and his mouth and his eyes kind of puckered up.

"I'm sorry, Tess. You're right. This is really dumb. We can go back to your dining room and work on barn owls." He jammed the pencil into his pocket and rolled the notebook up tight in his hands.

I kicked at a pile of leaves in the gutter. "Oh, all right," I said, finally. "But just Valu-Drug. No more."

Phoenix pulled out the pencil and unrolled the notebook. "Just Valu-Drug. No more," he said."Let's hurry."

We ran all the way to the shopping center. When we got onto the sidewalk in front of the Safeway, I slowed to a walk. Phoenix kept on running. I scanned the parking lot. No cars I knew, except maybe for the red one in front of Valu-Drug. It looked familiar, kind of. In fact, it kind of looked like Mrs. Field-Eaton's new car, but maybe this one was bigger? Why didn't I pay more attention to stuff like that?

Phoenix was peeking into store windows, probably leaving smudges from his hands and his nose. He passed the shoe repair and the hardware store and the laundromat.

Did Mrs. Field-Eaton's car have those buggy-looking headlights? I really couldn't remember.

"She's in here!" Phoenix shouted. He had his face pressed to the window of Valu-Drug. I didn't know why he sounded so surprised. People turned to look at him. I turned to read a sign about a lost dog taped on the laundromat's door.

Phoenix hauled open the door of Valu-Drug and went inside.

I walked over and looked at the displays of aspirin bottles and perfume in the window.

Phoenix poked his head out the door. "Hurry up, Tess."

I didn't move.

"Young man." The lady at the cash register was waggling a finger. "You're letting all the warm air out."

"Are you coming, Tess?"

Phoenix was still holding the door open. A man was waiting to go inside. The lady was coming around the check-out counter. People waiting at the cash register were watching.

I ducked past the man and shoved Phoenix inside. A wave of warm, popcorn-scented air hit me.

"This way," Phoenix whispered. He disappeared behind a stack of half-price Easter candy.

The lady was frowning at me. I smiled and walked around a big display of stuffed animals wearing T-shirts.

I walked right into Melissa Field-Eaton.

Mouthwash and Greeting Cards

"Tess! What are you doing here?"

"Uh . . . uh . . ."

Melissa held up a little white teddy bear holding a tiny bottle of perfume. "I'm getting a birthday present for my grandmother. I figure she'll keep the perfume and probably give the bear to me. Neat, huh?" She was chewing grape gum. I could smell it.

"Yeah. Great. Really special." I saw Phoenix's

head poke out from behind a stack of shampoo bottles.

"I gotta go, Melissa." I ducked around a shelf of china pigs into the next aisle. Melissa followed me.

"What are you looking for?" she asked.

"I have to get something for my mother." I grabbed a box off a shelf. "She needs this."

Melissa took the box from me. "Your mother's going to dye her hair?" She turned the box over. "Midnight Madness," she read out loud. "Wow, Tess, you are so lucky. I wish my mother would do stuff like this."

Phoenix came tromping down the aisle. He was writing in the notebook. "I found her," he said, wagging the pencil at us. "But now I've lost her." He looked up and down the aisle.

"She's not here," I said. I smiled and rolled my eyes at Melissa.

Phoenix pointed with the pencil. "I'll try acne medicine." His boots left muddy tracks as he walked away.

Melissa shook her head. "How embarrassing," she said. "I can't believe they let him out in public."

"No kidding." I felt my face getting hot. "Totally

embarrassing. Look, Melissa, I . . ."

Phoenix appeared at the other end of the aisle. "Not in acne. Have you seen her, Tess?"

Melissa looked at Phoenix. She looked at me.

"Band-Aids! I think I saw her in Band-Aids!" I shouted.

"Band-Aids!" Phoenix shouted back and clumped away again.

Melissa was still looking at me. Slowly, a big purple bubble grew out from between her lips.

"His mother," I said. "He's looking for his mother."

The bubble popped and Melissa sucked the gum back into her mouth. She nodded her head. "His mother."

"His mother."

"Aren't you guys supposed to be working on your science report?"

"Well. We were. We were supposed to do that. But, then, Phoenix had to go to the store."

"With his mother."

"Right. With his mother. Look, I really have to go, Melissa. My mother needs this stuff right now. Her hair is getting grayer by the minute."

I started toward the cash register. At the end of the aisle, I stopped and looked back. Melissa was just standing there, looking at me, stroking the teddy bear.

I headed for the nearest exit as fast as I could. Barn owls are not as bad as having the entire school know I was in Valu-Drug with Phoenix Guber.

As I reached the popcorn machine, a hand grabbed my sleeve.

Phoenix pulled me into the shampoo aisle. "I found her!" he whispered. "Come on."

He had dragged me past shampoo and through mouthwash before I managed to get my arm free. "Phoenix. I've gotta go. . . ." I turned and saw Melissa, right by the door, looking at a box of chocolate-creme eggs.

I ducked down and ran into the deodorant aisle. Phoenix was right behind me. "Gee, Tess," he whispered. "You should be a spy."

At the end of the aisle, he stopped, looked both ways, then dashed across into greeting cards. I followed him. There was another exit on this side, just behind the magazine rack. I prayed that Melissa wasn't going to get her grandmother something to read.

Phoenix was crouched down beside a rack of birthday cards. I stuffed the bottle of hair dye behind a card that said "Over the Hill." Phoenix peeked around the side, then jerked back, and started writing something down. He was having a great time. Collecting data. Keeping complete records so some other scientist could duplicate his research.

The magazine rack was around the corner. I checked to see if the coast was clear. Jane was standing there, reading a magazine. And right beside her was Melissa's brother, Robert.

I leapt back and nearly bumped into a little old lady who was reading get-well cards. "You should be more careful, little girl." She poked me once with her umbrella, and walked away.

"Isn't it incredible?" Phoenix asked. "Did you see what she's reading?"

"Did you see who she's standing next to?"

"That's not important, Tess. Look at what she's reading. I think this is an interesting development."

"It's probably just *Seventeen*," I said, looking again.

She wasn't reading *Seventeen*. She was reading *Astronomy*. My sister who had nearly flunked math two years in a row. My sister who couldn't find the moon on a clear night. My sister was reading a copy of *Astronomy* magazine.

I looked down at Phoenix. He was grinning so much his glasses were shoved up his face. "Working in the field is always suprising," he whispered.

I looked back at Jane. She was looking right back at me. And she wasn't grinning.

Robert had spotted us, too. At least he was smiling.

"Phoenix! Come here and look at this incredible picture of the Sombrero Galaxy!"

Phoenix tucked the notebook under his arm and sort of sidled over to Robert. Jane's eyes were wide open. So was her mouth. I'd never seen quite so much of Jane's braces before.

Melissa came around the corner from foot spray. All the Field-Eatons have curly, dark brown hair and big, dark brown eyes. I wondered if I would like Jane better if we looked more alike.

Melissa smiled at Jane. She frowned at me. "I thought you had to get home," she said. She ignored Phoenix completely. "Come on, Robert. Let's go."

"Well, it's about time." Robert put his magazine back on the rack. "You need a ride, Phoenix?"

Phoenix looked at Jane. "Uh . . . sure. I think I've collected all the data I can right now."

Robert laughed. "Data? Are you conducting an experiment in a drugstore?"

Phoenix's eyes met mine. "It's a little too early to discuss my findings, Robert. But I did find a nice owl pellet today." He pulled it out of his pocket. Melissa made a gagging noise. Jane's mouth dropped open even farther.

"Great," Robert said. "You can tell me about it in the car."

"In the car?" Melissa put her hands on her hips. "He can't. His mother is here somewhere."

"She is?" Phoenix looked around.

Melissa narrowed her eyes at me. I smiled and shrugged.

"Look, Melissa," Robert said. "I told Mom I'd take you to the store. I didn't say I'd take you home. Phoenix, do you want a ride?"

Phoenix looked at his boots. "Uh. Sure. I guess." He looked at me, but I was looking at the cover of *Off-Road* magazine.

"Are you coming, Melissa, or are you walking?" Robert asked.

"I'm coming. I'm coming. But Tess needs a ride, too. And Jane."

We all looked at Jane. Her mouth was still open. Her skin was turning a truly ugly shade of dark red. Phoenix started to open the notebook, then stopped.

Jane's mouth clicked shut. She dropped the magazine onto a shelf. Then she turned and walked quickly toward the exit.

"Does she always act like that?" Robert asked.

Phoenix and I looked at each other.

"We'll find that out," Phoenix said, finally, and made a note in the book.

Stupid Little Kid Games

Melissa tried to get into the front seat of the car, but Robert told her to get in back or take a bus. Phoenix rode in front and he and Robert started talking about something called the Deep Sky Club.

"I thought you said he was with his mother," Melissa whispered, as we backed, very slowly, out of the parking space. Robert hasn't had his license very long and he drives like my grandmother.

I shrugged. "It looked like his mother."

Melissa scrunched down in the corner. "Well, I just hope nobody sees us," she said, and made a face at the back of Phoenix's head.

I scrunched down in my corner, too. I was kind of hoping the same thing, but I was also hoping that Phoenix wouldn't see the faces Melissa was making.

"You really have to see this eight-inch Dobsonian," Robert said. "Last week we found M42. You want me to drop you at home?"

"I'm actually supposed to be at Tess's house." Phoenix shot me a quick look over his shoulder. "We're working on a science report."

"What on?"

"Jane. . . . Barn owls."

"Jane's Barn Owls? Is that a new species?"

"Well, it's sort of complicated. Did I show you my owl pellet?"

Melissa leaned as close to me as her seat belt would let her. "What a goon," she whispered. "Poor Tess. I bet you've had some morning."

I shrugged again. It had been some morning.

Melissa blew a big bubble with her gum. "Did you see 'Space Pigs' this morning?"

I shook my head. "I've been pretty busy."

"Too bad. It was great." She poked me in the arm. "Don't forget to watch 'Captain Cosmo' this afternoon. I know I'm going to win this time."

"Are you two still entering those dumb contests that nut does between commercials?" Robert asked, looking at us in the rearview mirror.

"They're not dumb and we're going to win this one, aren't we, Tess?" Melissa popped another bubble and I remembered it must be close to lunchtime.

"Sure we are," I said, even though I didn't really believe it. Melissa and I had been entering "Captain Cosmo's Cosmic Contests" for at least a year and we'd never even won a coupon for a free cone at Humdinger. I mostly sent in my postcards because Melissa bugged me until I did. And I liked to watch the old science fiction movies he showed.

"Does he still wear that dumb costume made out of egg cartons?" Robert asked, cautiously steering the car around the corner onto my street.

"They're not egg cartons and it's not a costume," Melissa said. "It's a space suit. He's supposed to be from the planet Cosmopolitan."

Robert laughed and slapped his hand against the steering wheel. "Listen. If Captain Cosmo is from the planet Cosmopolitan, then I'm from the planet *Newsweek*."

The car stopped in front of my house.

"Thanks," I said. I climbed out and shut the door.

Phoenix was getting out of the front. "Remember," Robert said, "the meeting on Tuesday will be really interesting. We should have clear skies and I want you to see this telescope."

"I'll be there." Phoenix shut the door and stood beside me on the sidewalk. I shuffled back a few steps.

Melissa stuck her head out the window. "Don't forget!"

"I know. If Captain Cosmo reads your name, I'll call you."

"Me, too!" she shouted. The car pulled away. Melissa looked like she was riding in a limousine.

"Have you ever won anything?" Phoenix asked.

"No."

"Actually, that's sort of amazing. I mean, statistically. If Captain Cosmo gives out a prize at every commercial break and you've been entering your name for . . . how long?" He was opening the notebook and getting out his pencil.

"Phoenix. I don't want to talk about it. Okay?"

"Okay."

I started up the driveway. Phoenix had to jog a little to catch up.

"Uh, Tess. Do you think your mom is still mad?"

"I really don't care, Phoenix."

And I didn't. I was too embarrassed to care. In fact, I hoped my mother killed me because then I'd be out of my misery. I couldn't believe Melissa Field-Eaton had actually caught me in Valu-Drug with Phoenix Guber. She'd be thinking that I had wanted to be in Valu-Drug. She's be thinking I had gone in there voluntarily, that I'd actually been having a good time with Phoenix. And, even if that was maybe sort of true, well, that still didn't mean I wanted Melissa thinking it. I mean, Phoenix might be okay, sometimes, but I had just remembered that, basically, he was a goon.

My mother was coming downstairs as we came in the front door. "Aha! There you are!"

I took a step backward right onto Phoenix's foot. Maybe I did care if Mom was mad.

"I want to talk to you in the kitchen, Tess Anderson. Perhaps Phoenix would like to wait in the dining room and get some more work done on that science report."

Phoenix blushed and started pulling off his boots. "Sure, Mrs. Anderson."

As soon as the kitchen door closed behind us, my mother turned on me with her hands on her hips and her eyes narrowed down to little slits.

"Just what was this business in your sister's closet?" She was whispering. She sounded a lot like a snake, but I didn't tell her that.

I made my own eyes very big and round. "Well. It wasn't my idea, Mom. Really."

"I don't care whose idea it was, Tess." She was leaning close to me so she could whisper and be mad at the same time. "You have to learn to respect your sister's privacy. Phoenix is a guest in our house and it's your responsibility to make sure he knows our rules. Do you understand that?"

I thought about pointing out that I didn't know we had a specific rule about closets, but I didn't think it was such a good time to bring that up. So I just said "Yes," and looked very seriously at the tabletop.

Mom sighed. "I know Jane has been hard to live

with lately, Tess, but really, it will get better. You simply have to learn to get along."

She put her hand under my chin and pulled my head up. "You are sisters, you know."

"Kate! We'd better get going," Dad called.

Mom moved her hand up and fluffed my hair. "Look. I don't expect you guys to like each other but I do expect you to treat each other like human beings. Okay?"

"Okay."

"Kate. The first time we see this kid will be at his college graduation if you don't hurry."

Mom grabbed her purse off the back of a chair. "Dad and I are going to the hospital to see Mrs. Wilson's new baby. Jane is in charge and I don't want to hear about any trouble. Got that?"

"Yes. I'm sorry, Mom."

She smiled and shook her head. "Funny how they never cover this stuff in the parenting books." She picked up a plate of sandwiches from the counter. "I made these for you and Phoenix. There's cookies in the cupboard and milk in the refrigerator."

I grabbed the cookies and followed her into the dining room. She set the sandwiches down in front of Phoenix. He had one of the brown books open.

"I know you two will be working really hard this afternoon," Mom said.

"Oh, yes, Mrs. Anderson." Phoenix was nodding his head so hard his glasses would have fallen off if they hadn't been tied on.

"Real hard, Mom," I said.

She walked to the front door. "William," she said, "this baby will be a PhD candidate before we see it."

Dad came out of the living room. He pointed a finger at me. "Don't bug your sister," he said. He and Mom went out.

Phoenix sat back in his chair and closed the book. "What did she say to you?"

I sat down. I took out a cookie, pulled it apart, and licked the cream off the insides. "She said she didn't want any trouble." I put the cookie halves on the table. "And she said I should treat Jane like a human being." I took another cookie.

Phoenix picked up a sandwich and took a bite. "We are treating her like a human being. Sort of like a representative example of all human beings, in fact. In her age group."

I put the two new cookie halves on top of the first ones. "And we're supposed to respect her privacy."

Saying it really sort of made me mad. She treated me worse than she treated Oscar Wilde. She never gave me any privacy at all, not even in the bathroom. But I was always supposed to be nice to her, just because she was going through a phase.

Phoenix finished his sandwich and dusted the crumbs off his hands. "We do need more data. We don't have anywhere near enough information for an in-depth report."

"Or a shallow report."

The doorbell rang. Jane came bounding down the stairs and had yanked the door open before the bell was even done ringing. I could tell by her face it wasn't anybody important.

"Thanks, Mr. Borman. I'll tell Daddy you put the Weed-Eater in the garage."

She shut the door and turned to go back up the stairs. Then she caught sight of Phoenix and me. Her eyes got narrow just like Mom's.

I felt Phoenix kind of shrink down in his chair, but I just sat up straighter.

"You two," she said. She pointed a purple fingernail at us. "I don't know what you're up to, but it had better stop. I don't have time for stupid little-kid games. You'd just better leave the grown-ups in this house alone." She ran up the stairs.

I crumbled a cookie in my hand. I'd had just about enough of Jane and her phases.

Phoenix was writing in the notebook, adding to "Vocalization" and "Physical Characteristics." He stopped writing. "Do you have a portable tape recorder?" he asked.

"Why?"

He scratched under his cap. "Well, I don't want to upset your dad, but I think we have to bug her. I mean, really bug her. Just in the interests of research." Phoenix looked at me. "Of course, your parents might not think we're respecting her privacy."

Upstairs, Jane's stereo went on. Loud rock music made the ceiling vibrate. I felt like I was vibrating, too.

"What do you mean by bug her?"

"A lot of scientists use tape recorders in their

research so they can analyze vocalizations more closely. I thought it might be interesting to get a tape of her voice."

I would start respecting Jane's privacy as soon as she started respecting mine. "What do we need?"

"A tape recorder."

"We've got two. I'll go get them."

"I Love You, Tess"

"I think one will be enough, Tess," Phoenix said. "I just want to get some of the vocalizations on tape." He checked to see if the tape recorder was working. "We can do the analysis later."

"What will we be analyzing it for?"

"Oh, you know. Repeated sounds. Interesting use of language."

"Oh, Robby," I sighed, and laughed.

Phoenix nodded. "I'm really sorry I didn't think

of the tape recorder sooner. The closet would have been the perfect place." He looked thoughtful. "Of course, I never really dreamed she talked to herself. She might be up there, right now . . ."

"No way, Phoenix," I said, holding up my hands. "No more closets."

"I know. I know. We probably couldn't hear anything over the music, anyway."

"Right. She probably can't even hear herself. So, how are we going to work this?"

"Well, I was thinking, maybe when she's on the phone, we could use the extension. . . ."

I shook my head and licked the cream off another cookie. "Not a chance. She can tell when you lift up the extension." I knew this for a fact.

"I was afraid of that." Phoenix watched me add another level to my cookie tower. "I guess we'll just have to go with the hidden-microphone trick."

I looked at him. I wasn't sure I even wanted to know, but I had to ask. "What hidden-microphone trick?"

"We'll hide the tape recorder somewhere and leave it running." He held up a finger as if he'd just thought of something. "Actually, I think maybe it would be best if I hid with the recorder." He frowned a little. "You know, Tess, I don't think your sister likes me very much."

"She's funny that way," I said, and watched as he made a note under "Social Interactions."

"And, of course, you'll have to keep her talking," he added, as he finished writing.

"What? Why me?"

"Who else can do it, Tess? We just agreed I should hide, and I doubt we can rely on her talking to herself down here."

"Let me tell you, Phoenix, we can rely on her talking to herself more than we can rely on her talking to *me*."

"You'll think of something, Tess. You're really much more intelligent and resourceful than you seem, you know." He got up and walked into the living room. "I think this will work best for our purposes."

I followed him. He was staring at the couch like he was going to buy it or something.

"Look, Phoenix, no matter how intelligent I seem, I do know two things. One, I know Jane is not going to sit and talk to me. Two, I know she's not going to come into this living room. She's upstairs listening to rock music and playing with makeup. She could be up there for days."

Phoenix was pulling the couch out from the wall. "Do you think there's enough room?"

"There was plenty of room before you started moving the furniture around."

"I mean for me." He climbed over the back of the couch and scrunched down behind it. "Can you see me?"

"No. Of course I can't see you. Knock it off, Phoenix. I told you this won't work. And my mother's not going to like you moving the furniture around."

He popped his head back up. "I think if you get her talking about something she's interested in, you'll find she'll talk."

"My mother?"

"No, Jane!"

I plopped down in the armchair. "I refuse to talk about hair mousse and how fat her thighs are."

"Try talking about Robert Field-Eaton."

I crossed my arms and legs. "That's even worse.

Anyway, it doesn't make any difference, Phoenix, because I know for a fact she's not coming into this living room."

Upstairs, the rock music got louder and then quieter as the bedroom door was opened and shut. Footsteps sounded in the hall.

Phoenix ducked back down behind the couch.

The footsteps were on the stairs and then Jane appeared in the hall. "What are you doing? You'd better not be making a mess." She crossed the dining room and the kitchen door swung closed behind her.

"Psst. Psst."

I ran over and knelt on the couch so I could see over the back. Phoenix was lying on his stomach with the tape recorder next to his face. He didn't look very comfortable.

"Shut up," I whispered. "She's only in the kitchen."

Phoenix craned his neck a little so he could look over his shoulder. "You have to get her to sit on the couch. This mike isn't very powerful."

"Phoenix, if she catches us . . ."

The kitchen door creaked. I whirled around and sat.

Jane came into the living room. She was chewing on a carrot.

I didn't like the look in her eyes. Go back upstairs, I thought. Suddenly, Jane's privacy seemed a lot more important to me.

She came over and sat down beside me. Behind us, I heard a loud "click."

"Hi, Jane. How's it going?" I shouted.

She was leaning forward, rolling the carrot back and forth in her hands, acting like she hadn't even heard me, let alone the click. See, Phoenix? I thought. Jane won't talk to me.

Suddenly she sat up and turned toward me. I could see the little sparkly bits in her purple eye shadow. She looked very serious.

"Tess. I need to talk to you about something really important."

My mouth got dry.

"I really want to talk to you about how I feel about all the stuff that's happened today."

"About today?" I didn't want to talk to Jane about

today. I'd hidden in her closet with Phoenix Guber. I'd followed her to the drugstore with him. "Wouldn't you rather talk about mousse or ... or ..."

She held up her carrot. "Let me finish, Tess, because I've really thought a lot about this, you know, and I want you to know how I feel."

I knew how *I* was feeling. I was feeling sick. I wished she'd just say something mean and nasty like she usually did. If this was another phase, I hoped it would be over fast.

"I haven't been the best sister in the world in the past few months. I know that, Tess. I mean, sometimes I just don't know what happens. It's like my mouth opens and says things and I don't even know why. I mean, I don't plan to say awful things to you. Well, not all the time, anyway. I just sort of keep saying them and I can't stop."

I nodded, but I didn't say anything. I didn't want to interrupt her. I hoped Phoenix was getting this all on tape. This was almost an apology.

"Being a teenager isn't easy, Tess." She looked down at her carrot. "Things just seem to happen so fast and then there's school and everything. And I know that's no excuse for acting like a creep."

I nodded some more. She could keep on talking about herself. Just as long as she didn't talk about me. Just as long as she didn't talk about me and Phoenix.

She looked up at me. Tears were brimming against her lashes. I scrunched my eyes shut.

"But never, never, Tess, have I been as awful to you as you've been to me today."

My eyes jerked open. Oh, no. She was going to talk about me.

"I love you, Tess. I mean, even though I don't always act like it, I love you like . . . like a sister. And I never, ever dreamed that you would do something so awful, so nasty, so humiliating." The tears spilled out of her eyes.

I could feel my face getting hot, and a lump was growing in my throat. "Don't cry, Jane. You'll . . . your mascara will run."

She rubbed at her eyes and her mascara smudged all over instead. "Do you have any idea how embarrassed I was? I mean, I open my closet door and there's a boy in there. Tess, I was in my bathrobe. I had . . . I had green stuff all over my face. I'll never forget how I felt as long as I live."

I wished I could go away, disappear, vanish into thin air. I'd never humiliated anybody before. I'd never done anything they wouldn't forget for as long as they lived.

"I'm sorry, Jane. I really am." I was starting to cry, too.

She sat back and put her feet up on the coffee table. We both just sat there for a couple of minutes, Jane crying and me trying not to. Finally Jane sniffed a couple of loud sniffs. I wiped my own eyes and wished I had a tissue. Jane took a couple of deep, shaky breaths and wiped mascara on her pants.

"So, anyway, that's how I feel. Mom said I should tell you and maybe I'd feel better." She took another shaky breath and a bite of the carrot. "I'm glad I decided to talk to you. I do feel better."

"Great," I said. I, personally, felt awful.

Jane looked around the room like she'd just realized where she was. "Where is Phoenix, anyway?"

The lump in my throat dropped straight into my stomach. "Uh. Oh. He's around. Somewhere."

She bit off another chunk of carrot and stuck it

in her cheek so she could talk. "I mean, that's what I really didn't get about all of this. Why were you hanging around with Phoenix Guber in the first place? A science report is one thing, Tess, but sitting in my closet? Going to the store?" She shook her head and crunched the carrot. "I thought you hated him."

Sweat prickled into my bangs. "I never said that! I never said I hated him!"

Jane laughed. "Well, if that wasn't hating him, I don't know what was. You said he smelled. You said he tripped over his own feet. You said everybody called him Phoenix Boober."

I leapt up and nearly knocked over the coffee table. "I did not!" I shouted.

Jane blinked at me. "You did, too, Tess. You said he was a goon."

"That was different. That was last year."

"Tess. It was this morning."

There was another "click" behind the couch, followed by a rustling and thumping. Phoenix wiggled his way out and stood up. "I think I'd better be going," he said.

Jane shot off the couch like it had pinched her.

"Tess Anderson, you little snake! I'm going to kill you!"

Jane was heading toward me. Phoenix was heading toward the door. Everybody was mad at me and it wasn't even my fault. Well, not all my fault. I could feel the tears starting up again. This was all totally unfair.

The phone rang.

I Won!

The phone rang again. Jane stopped and stared at it. Phoenix stopped and stared at it.

It rang again and I grabbed it. Even talking to someone who wanted to shampoo the carpets would be better than facing everybody who was mad at me.

"Tess!" It was Melissa. She was screaming so loudly I had to pull the phone away. "Tess! What are you doing on the phone? Call them! Call them quick!"

"Call who?"

"Tess! You won! You won! Haven't you been watching? Hurry up. Call before it's too late! He's already said your name twice!" Melissa slammed the phone down in my ear.

I turned around. Phoenix was still standing in the doorway. Jane was still standing in front of the couch, clutching her carrot like a knife.

"I won," I said. I looked down at the phone. I'd won. I'd finally won. "I won!" I shrieked at the top of my lungs. I banged down the phone, grabbed Jane, and started dancing her around the coffee table. "I won, I won, I won!"

"What did you win?" Jane dragged me to a stop. "Quit acting like a jerk, Tess. What did you win?"

I stared up at her. "I don't know. It was on TV. On 'Captain Cosmo.' He read my name. Twice. . . . Oh, no!"

Phoenix beat me to the TV. Captain Cosmo's silver face glowed on the screen. "So that's the number, Tess Anderson. You only have three more minutes . . . oops, make that two minutes and fifty-eight seconds to call this station and claim your prize. And now . . . a Ritchie the Rodent cartoon!"

I screamed again. "I missed the number! I don't even know what I've won and now I'll never win it because I missed the number. Maybe it was the trip to Enchanted Mountain. Maybe it was the ten-speed bike. Maybe . . ."

Jane took a bite of her carrot and smiled. "Serves you right."

"Call Melissa," Phoenix said, quietly. "Maybe she knows the number."

My fingers were shaking so hard, I could barely dial the numbers. A loud "beep, beep" filled my ears. "Busy," I said.

"You have a minute and forty-six seconds," Phoenix said.

I grabbed Jane's arm. "Jane you've got to help me! Think of something! Quick!"

She pulled her arm loose. "I don't have to help you, Tess. After the way you treated me today, I hope they give your prize to Melissa!"

"I'm sorry, Jane. About everything. Really and truly. I'll never do it again." And I meant it.

She looked at Phoenix. "I'm sorry, too," he said. He didn't say what he was sorry about, exactly.

I put my hands together. "I'll make it up to you. I'll buy you new shampoo. I'll . . ." I thought frantically. "I'll clean the cat box."

Jane pointed the carrot at me. "For a month. You clean the cat box for a whole month."

On the TV, the little rodents were cheering for Ritchie. The cartoon was almost over.

"Sure. Fine. Anything."

She dropped the carrot in the ashtray. "What are the call letters of that TV station?"

"Call letters?"

"You know. When they say, 'You are watching KZBC,' or something like that."

"I don't know." But I should know. I must have heard that a thousand times. "Wait a minute. Wait a minute. I think it begins with a *K*."

Jane moaned. "Wonderful. They all start with *K* around here, dimwit. You spend half your life in front of that tube and you don't even know that?" She looked at Phoenix. "Do you know?"

"Sorry. I'm not allowed to watch commercial television."

"Parents!" Jane said. "Well, I'll just call information."

I held my breath and watched her dial.

"Portland, Oregon," she said. "Yes. Could you please give me the number of Channel Twelve?"

I clenched my hands so hard, my fingernails cut into my palms.

"555-4575." I saw Phoenix writing it in his notebook.

"Thank you very much," Jane said. She swung around. She was grinning. "Hurry up, Tess!" she shouted.

"555-4575," Phoenix said. "Thirty seconds."

I leapt up, grabbed the phone, and dialed. "It's ringing," I whispered.

It rang again. And again. And again.

"Ten seconds," Phoenix whispered.

Another ring.

"Did you dial wrong, Tess?" Jane asked.

I didn't know. I couldn't have. Could I?

"Good afternoon," a woman said. "This is KWOW. May I help you?"

"Yes!" I shouted. "This is me! I mean, this is Tess Anderson. I won!"

"Oh, yes. Tess Anderson. I've been waiting for you to call." She didn't sound very glad to hear from me. "It looks like you made it just in time. Now, is there an adult I can speak to?"

I put my hand over the mouthpiece. "She wants to talk to an adult."

"Give it to me." Jane coughed a couple of times. She stood up straighter. Then she took the phone. "Hello? I'm the person in charge."

I tried to stand close so I could hear, too, but Jane frowned, and I moved away.

"Yes, I understand. Thank you very much." Jane gave a big sigh and stuck her tongue out at the phone. "What a jerk."

"What did she say? What did she say?" I was jumping up and down.

"She said you can pick up your prize today before three or from nine to six on any weekday, but it has to be before Friday. I think she just wanted to make sure that a responsible person heard the instructions."

"So, what did you win, Tess?" Phoenix asked.

"I don't know. What did I win, Jane?"

"I don't know. She just told me when you could

pick it up. I thought she told you what it was." Jane shook her head. "You're unbelievable, Tess."

"And I'm sure that somewhere out there in the known universe, Tess Anderson will be very happy with that prize." Captain Cosmo was smiling from Cosmopolitan again.

"What prize?" I shouted at the TV. "What prize?"

"Now, why did the Martian cross the road?" Phoenix turned off the TV.

I turned to Jane. "Can we go downtown? Right now?" Mom didn't get home from work until five on weekdays. I might never get my prize!

"Tess." Jane had that grown-up voice again. "The station is in northeast Portland. It would take us an hour on the bus. And Mom and Dad won't be home until three at least."

"It's no fair!" I shouted. "For the first time in my whole life, I've finally won something and I'll never even get to see what it is."

"Tess. Read my lips. There is no way we can get downtown in time today."

"I could ask Robert," Phoenix said. "He drives me to the Deep Sky Club all the time."

"Yes, yes, yes!" I shouted. But I bet Phoenix could

barely hear me because Jane was shouting: "No, no, no!"

Phoenix and I both stared at her. She blushed. "I mean. Well. My hair's a mess. And I don't have anything to wear."

"You don't have to come," I said, pushing Phoenix toward the phone.

Her face turned an even brighter shade of red. "Oh, Tess. I can't let you go alone. Mom would never forgive me if I let you go alone."

I started to point out that I wasn't exactly going alone, but she was already halfway up the stairs. "Give me two minutes!" she shouted.

Jane came down just as Robert pulled into the driveway. She'd found something to wear and she'd done something to her hair. Something red.

"Come on! Come on! Hurry up!" I was dancing around in the hall. I knew we were going to be late. I just knew it.

Jane snapped her fingers. "A key. I have to get a key to the house." She went into the kitchen.

Phoenix was writing something in his notebook. He ripped the page out. "Here," he said, "it's the address of the television station. I looked it up for you."

"You keep it," I said. "I'll probably just drop it or something."

Phoenix pushed the paper at me again. "You keep it, Tess. I have to go home."

I stopped jumping around. "Aw, Phoenix. Come on."

He looked down at the floor. He had a hole in his sock I hadn't noticed before. "No. I really have to be going."

Outside, Robert beeped the horn.

"Phoenix, you have to come." I waved the note he'd given me. "Look. I can't even read this. Is this a three or a five?"

"It's a seven."

"See? We'll just get totally lost without you. And what if Jane does something interesting? Who's going to write it down?"

The horn beeped again.

"Come on!" I grabbed his arm and managed to drag him out onto the porch. I left him putting on his boots and I jumped down the stairs.

Robert was sitting in the front seat. Melissa was sitting in the back. Somehow, I'd sort of forgotten all about her. I stopped dead at the foot of the porch steps. Phoenix ploughed right into me.

"Ow!" he said. Then, "Oh," when he saw Melissa.

I walked right up to the car, opened the door, and climbed in beside Melissa. "Hi!" I said with a big smile. "Pretty exciting, huh?"

Melissa didn't say anything. She was staring at Phoenix, who was still standing on the sidewalk. Robert didn't say anything, either. He was staring at Jane, who was climbing in beside me. He looked like he'd never seen her before. Or anything quite like her.

"Let's go!" Melissa said, kicking the back of the front seat.

Robert turned around and started the motor.

"Wait!" I leaned over Jane and rolled down the window. "Come on, Phoenix!" I shouted.

He just stood there, rolling and unrolling his notebook. "I do need to get home."

"Phoenix," I said. "I bet we only have something like twenty-two minutes and forty-five seconds left. Get in the car."

He looked from me to Melissa, and back to me again. "Well, okay." He got in beside Robert.

"So," Robert said. "Who knows where we're going?"

"I wrote the address down here," Phoenix said.

"I wrote the address down here," Melissa repeated, in a not-very-quiet, not-very-nice voice.

I poked her in the ribs with my elbow.

"Why is he here?" she whispered in my ear.

In the front, I saw Phoenix's head go down and his shoulders go up. "Because he's helping me," I whispered back. "And . . . and because I asked him," I added, a little louder.

She raised her eyebrows and turned to look out the window, like she didn't want to hear any more about it.

That was okay with me. I didn't want to talk to her, anyway. I looked at Jane. Her lips were moving, like she was saying something over and over. I watched and she did it for a couple of minutes. Then, so suddenly I jumped, she said: "Well, hasn't the weather been just great?" very loudly. It came out real fast and all run together, like she was afraid she was going to forget it or something. Then her face turned red and she looked out the window, too.

No one answered her. We just drove, in complete silence, for what seemed like a long time. I wanted to ask Phoenix what time it was, but I was afraid to know. I wanted to ask Melissa what I'd won, but I was afraid she'd just say something mean to Phoenix.

Finally, we slowed down in front of a big white building with the letters KWOW written in red on the side. "This is it," Robert said.

We got a parking place right in front of the building and we all trooped inside. A lady with stiff blond hair was sitting behind a big, white desk, reading a magazine.

"May I help you?" she asked, looking up at Robert. He shook his head and pointed at me.

I stepped forward. "I'm Tess Anderson. I've come to collect my prize from Captain Cosmo." I pointed to the picture of him on the wall behind her desk. It was right next to a picture of Clint Harmon. I wondered if Jane saw it, but she was looking at the plant in the corner.

The lady said something into a machine on her

desk. "He'll be out in a minute," she said, and went back to reading her magazine.

A man came out of a door down the hall and walked toward us. He had hair like my father's: a lot on the sides and not much on the top. He was wearing a bright green T-shirt that said ARE WE HAVING FUN YET? His stomach made a big bulge under the words. He looked sort of familiar, but I couldn't remember where I'd seen him before. Behind me, Melissa giggled.

"Which one of you is Tess Anderson?" he asked.

"Uh . . . I am," I said.

"Here's your prize," he said. He held out a flat, skinny envelope.

I just stared at it.

"Take it, Tess," Jane hissed from behind the plant.

I didn't move. "I thought Captain Cosmo was going to give it to me," I said, finally.

The man smiled. The lady behind the desk laughed. Jane groaned.

"I am Captain Cosmo," the man said. "I'm on my way home." He leaned a little closer to me. "They don't let me wear the costume out of the studio."

I nodded.

He flapped the envelope at me. "It's four tickets to the Ice Extravaganza. Congratulations."

I nodded again. I had known it wasn't the ten-speed. Or even tickets to Enchanted Mountain. Nothing exciting came in an envelope that skinny.

"Take it, Tess," Jane whispered again.

I took the envelope. "Say thank you, Tess," Jane hissed.

"Thank you," I said.

"My pleasure," Captain Cosmo said. "Enjoy the show."

As Robert drove the car away from the curb, Melissa said: "I think that's great, Tess. Enchanted Mountain isn't that big a deal."

"Yeah," Robert said. "Too many crowds. Long lines. You'd hate it there."

Phoenix turned around. "Can I see the tickets, Tess?"

I handed them over.

"Wow," he said. "Front-row seats for this Friday. Do you know what the show is this year?"

I shook my head.

"Journey to Another Planet. The special effects are supposed to be amazing. My dad tried to get tickets, but they've been sold out for weeks." Carefully he slipped my tickets back into the envelope. "You're really lucky, Tess."

Melissa took the envelope from Phoenix. "Four tickets. That's great. I can probably come with you. I'm not doing anything Friday night."

I took the envelope and stuffed it in my pocket. I tried to forget about the ten-speed and Enchanted Mountain.

Robert looked back, really quickly. He shrugged. Then he smiled at Jane.

Jane made a funny little noise. Then she smiled at me. Gently, she punched me on the shoulder. "Come on," she said. "It's better than not winning anything at all."

"I guess." I punched her back. Then I grinned. "At least it's better than a coupon to Humdinger."

Not Too Mushy

Robert pulled the car into our driveway. "Thanks, Robert," I said, as I got out.

"Any time, Tess. Call me when you win again." He looked at Phoenix. "You need a ride home?"

Melissa made a face. "I guess so," Phoenix said. He looked at me. "I have some data I need to review."

Jane was standing on the sidewalk, staring at the car. Suddenly, she stuck her head in Phoenix's window. "My name's Jane. Jane Anderson."

Robert nodded. "I know. I've seen you around school."

She nodded. "Me, too," she said. She stepped back from the car.

Melissa scooted over and stuck her head out the window. "I'm glad you won, Tess," she said. "Remember, I can go Friday."

I nodded and waved. I saw Phoenix had his notebook out. I pointed to it. "Thanks for helping," I said.

At the end of the driveway, Robert and Melissa waved. Phoenix didn't even look up.

I heard a deep, heavy sigh beside me.

Jane was watching the car go down the street. "I really think it's a good thing to have a short first name, don't you?" she said, suddenly.

"What?"

"I mean, I think short first names sound better with long last names."

"Like Anderson?"

"Uh-huh. And Field-Eaton." Jane started toward the front porch. She had this funny, blank look on her face.

In the house, she went straight up to her room. I tucked the envelope inside the gravy boat in the china cabinet, where Mom and Dad keep important mail. I stood there, looking at Phoenix's books still spread all over the dining-room table. I scooped up the cookie pieces and threw them in the garbage in the kitchen. Then I followed Jane upstairs.

The door to her bedroom was open, so I went in. She was sitting at her desk. A can of red styling mousse was open in front of her. A pile of sweaters was on the floor by her chair.

I sat down on the edge of the bed. Oscar Wilde jumped off and curled up on the sweaters. I stuck my tongue out at him. He yawned and I could smell his cat-food breath.

Jane was staring very closely at her nose. "You want something?" she asked.

"I was just thinking what a weird day it's been. I mean, the closet and the drugstore and all that."

Jane poked at something on her nose. "What was that all about, anyway?"

I took a deep breath and let it out very slowly. "I don't know. It was just a dumb idea."

"Dumb isn't the word for it." She looked at me. "Although I have to admit, this whole thing with you and Phoenix turned out a lot better than I expected, Tess." Her eyes unfocused and she rubbed her hand on her nose. "I may not want to forget this day after all."

She was right. This whole thing had turned out better than I had expected, too. Parts of it, anyway.

"What are you looking at?" I went over to the desk and leaned closer to the mirror.

"My pores. I've been trying this new stuff to shrink them." Jane held up a small white jar and unscrewed the lid. "Here it is. It's supposed to be murder on zits, too."

It looked like a jar of mud. Thick, wet mud. I started to stick my finger in, but she jerked the jar away. "Careful! It's expensive. It cost me most of my baby-sitting money for a month." She held up a tube of something else. "Now this tightens your skin." She squeezed a tiny bit out on her fingertip. It was bright, shiny green. "Keeps you from getting wrinkles."

"You don't have wrinkles," I said.

"And I'm not going to get them, either." She looked at the green stuff on her finger, then wiped it on her jeans.

"What's this?" I picked up a big blue jar with no label.

"Oh. That's for peely feet. I bought it by mistake." She started digging in a little paper bag. *Valu-Drug* was written across the side. "I just got this today." She held up a mascara, still in its cardboard-and-plastic package. She opened it and threw the wrapping on the floor. "It's scented," she said, waving the inky-looking mascara wand under my nose.

"It makes your eyelashes smell?"

"Yeah. Pretty stunning, huh?"

She leaned closer to the mirror, opened her eyes very wide, and started applying the mascara to her eyelashes.

"Jane."

Our eyes met in the mirror again. Her hand stayed in midair, about half an inch from her eyes. "Yeah?"

"I just want to thank you for helping me this afternoon. And . . . and I want you to know . . . I love you, too."

She blinked and some of the mascara smudged onto her cheek.

"Don't get too mushy, okay?" she said, finally.

"Okay. Do you want to come to the Ice Extravaganza?"

She started turning her head from side to side, studying her reflection. "I think I may be busy Friday night, Pest." She applied a little more mascara to her left eye. Then she dropped the mascara and grabbed the blue jar I was still holding. "How many times do I have to tell you to leave my stuff alone?"

I grinned. "Gee, Jane, it's great to see your phases back to normal."

Downstairs, the front door opened. "Anybody home?" Dad shouted.

"We are," I shouted back. "And I won!"

As I ran out into the hall, Jane yelled, "And don't forget the cat box!"

I showed Mom and Dad the tickets. "That's wonderful, Tess," Mom said, giving me a hug.

"There are four, see," I said. "We could all go, but Jane doesn't want to, so can you both come?"

Mom made a face. "Sweetie, I'm sorry but I can't. I have a meeting that night."

"But I will be delighted to attend." Dad gave a sweeping little bow. "Ask Miss Field-Eaton and another of your friends and we'll make a night of it. Burgers and shakes at Humdinger on me."

"Okay," I said, slowly. "I guess I could ask Erica or Brianne."

The doorbell rang. "That's probably Melissa now," Mom said. She and Dad went into the kitchen.

But it was Phoenix again.

"I forgot my books," he said.

"Come on in."

He'd changed into sneakers with Velcro fasteners, but he still had his cap and the backpack. He started stuffing books into it.

I found a loose thread in the tablecloth and pulled at it. "I'm sorry, Phoenix," I said. Boy, I'd never apologized to so many people in one day in my whole life.

He kept on stuffing books. "You don't have to apologize, Tess."

"I want to, Phoenix. I mean, you know, for all that stuff Jane said I said."

He looked at me for a minute and I blushed. "For

all that stuff I said," I said, finally.

"I know what everybody at school says about me, Tess. I know they call me Phoenix Boober. I know they all hate me."

"Everybody doesn't hate you, Phoenix."

"Yeah? Name one."

I picked up a book. "I don't hate you. I mean, well, maybe I didn't like you a whole lot before, but I didn't know you, either. I mean, I like you now. Now that I know you."

He had a book in each hand, like he was going to juggle them or something. "I like you, too, Tess," he said. "I actually had a pretty good time today." He sounded surprised.

He put down one of the books and adjusted his glasses. For the first time, I noticed he had hazel eyes, too. "You know, I wasn't very happy about this assignment. I thought it was really mean of Mr. Sanders to team me up with such a featherbrained partner. My mother had to force me to come over here this morning. She kept saying it would be good for me."

"What?" Featherbrained? Featherbrained? "I'm not featherbrained!"

"I know that now, Tess." Phoenix was nodding. "Now that I know you."

I ruffled the pages of the book I was holding. "What are we going to do about our report? I sort of don't feel like doing it on Jane anymore."

"I figured you'd say that. I'm not sure we ever could have organized all that data, anyway. Our subject may have been a little too complex."

"Or a little too crazy," I said.

We grinned at each other.

I snapped the book shut. "I guess we're back to all these books, huh?"

Phoenix shook his head. He was grinning even more. "Actually, I know all this stuff already, Tess. I did a report on barn owls for a TAG class last year. I just brought these along to make you suffer. Most of them aren't even about owls."

I put my hands on my hips. "Phoenix Guber! What a rotten thing to do."

He nodded happily. "You're right. Pretty rotten." He dug into his pocket and pulled out the owl pellet. "We still have this. I'm going to soak the fur off and find out what's inside. You want to help?"

I looked at the fuzzy wad. It still looked disgusting.

"You know, Tess, sometimes you can find the entire skeleton of a . . ."

"Small mammal. I know. I know. I heard that before." I looked more closely at the pellet. It looked like it was sealed up, kind of like a neat little package. There were really bones in that thing? "Sure, Phoenix. I'd like to help. It sounds like fun." And, in a funny kind of way, it did sound like fun.

I got my jacket and told my parents where I was going. They looked sort of surprised, but all my dad said was, "Stay out of closets."

As we were walking down the porch steps, I said, very fast, before I could think too much about it: "You want to come to the Ice Extravaganza with my dad and Melissa and me?"

Phoenix stopped on the bottom step and stared at me. "What about Jane?"

"She's hoping she's going to be busy."

"But what about Melissa? She won't like it."

"Phoenix. This is not a multiple-choice question. Do you want to come or don't you?"

"You're not just asking me because of today? You really want me to come and you're not just being nice?"

I could see myself in his glasses. "Look. I am not being nice. I really want you to come to the Ice Extravaganza because I like you. And Melissa will like you, too." Once she gets over the shock, I thought. "Once she gets to know you," I said.

One of his books started slipping, but Phoenix juggled it back with his knee. "I'd like to come, Tess. I'd like that a lot." He was smiling. Phoenix Guber, when he smiles, does not look half bad.

ABOUT THE AUTHOR

"I always wanted to be a writer because people thought I was crazy when I talked to myself," says Margaret Bechard. "This book grew out of my memories of being a younger sister, combined with the time my oldest son won a coloring contest sponsored by a local TV station, mixed in with the day I announced that I absolutely would not have a shoe box filled with owl pellets, fur, and bones on the shelf in the family room. The rest I just made up as I got to know Tess and Phoenix better."

Margaret Bechard, the youngest of six children, grew up in Chico, California. A graduate of Reed College, she lives in Tigard, Oregon. "I am married to Lee Boekelheide, a software engineer who would rather be an astronomer," she says, "and we have three sons, the last time I checked." *My Sister, My Science Report* is Ms. Bechard's first book.